GRISEL AND THE
TOOTH FAIRY
& OTHER STORIES

By the same author:

Butterfingers
Get Lavinia Goodbody!
Hanky-Panky
Paper Flags and Penny Ices
Sticky Fingers
Willy and the Semolina Pudding
and Other Stories
Willy and the UFO and Other Stories

GRISEL AND THE TOOTH FAIRY
& OTHER STORIES

ROGER COLLINSON

Illustrated by TONY ROSS

Andersen Press · London

First published in 1998 by
Andersen Press Limited,
20 Vauxhall Bridge Road, London SW1V 2SA

British Library Cataloguing in Publication Data available
ISBN 0 86264 689 8

Phototypeset by Intype London Ltd
Printed and bound in Great Britain by
the Guernsey Press Co. Ltd., Guernsey, Channel Islands

Contents

1 Grisel and the Tooth Fairy   7

2 Grisel and the School Hat   15

3 Grisel and the Pantomime   24

4 Grisel and the Easter Eggs   33

5 Grisel and the Nativity Play   42

6 Grisel and the Orange Drizzle Cake   51

7 Grisel and Little Tristram   61

8 Grisel and the Three Wishes   72

1

Grisel and the Tooth Fairy

Grisel was short of cash. Grisel was *always* short of cash. One of Grisel's Granny's sayings was *The best things in life are free.* But until the day comes when shopkeepers dish out sweets, ice-creams and sticky buns for nothing, Grisel's opinion is that Granny talked a load of cod's-wallop.

Grisel, I repeat, was short of cash; and the particular occasion was the Brownies' outing to Southend-on-Sea. The coach was to be free; the picnic lunch was to be free; a tea of burgers and French fries at McDonald's was to be free; and Mum had already promised Grisel a packet of her favourite sweets for free. So why, you ask, this desperate need for cash? The answer to that is another question: were the slot machines in the amusement arcades free? – They were *not*! So Grisel needed silver coins, as many as she could lay her hands on, because slot machines can gobble up a fortune without a single burp. But, on the other hand, Grisel knew that these same machines would sometimes give you back not just pennies but pounds and pounds. For a mere fifty p., if you were very lucky, you might win untold riches. They called it 'hitting the jackpot'. True, there was a chance – Grisel had to face it – that she might lose all and come away with nothing. But it was a chance she was prepared to take. She knew she had to risk losing what she'd got in order to get her hands on a lot more of the stuff. Except Grisel hadn't got any in the first place. Which brings me back to where I was at the beginning.

The outing was only a day or two away, and Grisel had still not raised a bean. All her birthday money had gone a fortnight before in an orgy of spending; and she'd already blown an advance of three weeks' pocket money on a special offer in her comic of a monster mask; and Granny and her purse were both away visiting Auntie Vivienne. Grisel was quite prepared to do paid work; but no one would give her jobs. They all said it would be quicker, safer, and cheaper to do them for themselves. The world, Grisel concluded, was full of pigs. She had searched for money. She had fished down the sides of the armchairs and the sofa, but had found nothing of greater value than hair-grips and assorted biscuit crumbs. It was maddening. Wealth was waiting there in Southend's arcade machines – wealth for the taking – but lost to her for want of a handful of small change.

Grisel was musing bitterly on Life when she bit

upon a piece of crackling from the roast pork which Mum had cooked for dinner. And, as she bit, she felt a twinge in one of her top, front teeth. She winced, and gingerly she bit again. Again a nasty twinge. Grisel took the crackling from her mouth and explored the tooth with her tongue. It wobbled – not a lot – but it definitely wobbled. Alas, to add to all her other woes, a tooth was loose. A girl couldn't even enjoy the simple pleasure of chewing at a bit of crackling! And then it was that a great light shone, as it dawned on Grisel that her gums' loss would be her pocket's gain. For, you see, the Tooth Fairy still came to Grisel's house by night and bought up her discarded teeth at fifty p. a go.

9

What use the Fairy had for them was no one's business but her own; and, provided the fifty p. was under her pillow in the morning, Grisel didn't care.

The tip of her tongue continued to probe what she now realised could be the source of badly needed capital. But the wobbly tooth was worthless while it remained there in her head. The Tooth Fairy's deals were strictly cash-in-hand, and she never left an I.O.U. But, by the same token, she only paid out for teeth-in-hand. The Brownies' outing was on Saturday; today was Thursday. A wobbly tooth, left to itself, could wobble on for days and days. This one was going to need encouragement.

When she was allowed to get down from the table, Grisel hurried to her special place behind the toolshed at the bottom of her garden, and there she set to work. First, she got the tooth between her thumb and forefinger and levered at it. It seemed firmer than before; but Grisel continued to apply a steady pressure. She pushed at that tooth, backwards and forwards; and it hurt her quite a lot. But, with fifty p. as the reward for a Do-It-Yourself extraction, Grisel persevered. *No gain without pain* was another of Granny's sayings; and Grisel thought that, this time, the old trout had got it right.

All through the afternoon, Grisel worked at it; and, by four o'clock, the tooth was very loose indeed. It hung there like a cat-flap in her smile. The time had come to stop the pushing and the pulling and to begin the twisting. At first, the tooth revolved about a quarter turn; but, just before she was called in to tea, it was held in place only by a thread of root. Grisel twisted until, at last, the tooth broke free and she held it in her palm – a hard-earned fifty p.'s worth. The gap in the front of her mouth felt a bit funny; and her big sister, Hildegard, would have died rather than appear gap-toothed in public. But Grisel cared little for appearances. What were looks compared with cash and the goodies it could buy? She pranced back to the house to find the family already seated at the tea table. 'My toof's come out!' she lisped, triumphantly; and she held up the evidence for inspection, at the same time pointing to the vacancy in her delighted beam.

'Ugh!' Hildegard shuddered.

'You didn't say your tooth was loose,' said Mum.

'I expect the Toof Fairy will come tonight,' Grisel answered, ignoring Mum's remark.

Mum and Dad looked at each other with raised eyebrows.

'That tooth,' said Grisel's mum, 'just when did you first know that it was loose?'

'I bet I know,' Hildegard interrupted. 'She went all funny at dinnertime. She took some crackling out of her mouth, and you could see she was poking about with her tongue.'

Grisel poked the tongue out at sister Hildegard.

'And that's enough of that!' Mum said sharply.

11

'*Well*!' protested Grisel.

'How did that tooth come out so quickly?' Mum asked. 'You've not been pulling at it, have you . . . ? That's not what you've been up to all the afternoon?'

Grisel's lower lip stuck out in stubborn silence.

'Ugh!' Hildegard shuddered for the second time. 'Imagine! Pulling out your own teeth to make money! She's like something in a horror film!'

Grisel glared at Hildegard. And it was fortunate for Hildegard that the Tooth Fairy did not pay you for other people's teeth.

'Don't you ever do that again,' Mum said, sternly. And then, in gentler tones, 'It must have hurt you dreadfully.'

Grisel passed the hours after tea in quiet content, assured that, in the morning, she would have her fifty p. Not a lot, but enough for a flutter on the slot machines. Her self-inflicted sufferings would be recompensed.

Granny, as well as being the dispenser of unwanted wisdom and advice, also produced the most delicious home-made toffee. All pure cream and butter, the great mouth-watering chunks were studded with nuts and raisins. With a bit of Granny's toffee in your mouth, speech was impossible. At those times, when all the family were chewing, an unnatural silence would fall upon the house. During

12

the evening, the tin was opened and everybody took a piece. Greedily, Grisel helped herself to an enormous lump and began to chew. At once, she felt a twinge such as she had felt at dinnertime, but much more painful. She would have cried out, but her jaws were stuck together. And, when she did manage to prise them apart and remove the toffee, there, imbedded in it with the nuts and raisins, was a tooth. The *same* tooth which had hurt when she had bitten on the crackling. And then it was that Grisel understood that she had spent the afternoon in pulling out the wrong tooth! All that pain! And now a huge gap which even she felt to be grotesque. Grisel dissolved in tears.

Dad, insensitive to his younger daughter's grief, only observed: 'When the cameraman says *Cheese!* on the Brownies' outing, you'd better keep your mouth shut.'

But Mum said: 'Give me that toffee, you poor lamb. I'll throw it in the bin.'

It was two o'clock in the morning when Mum and Dad and Hildegard were wakened by a noise from down below. Was it the cat? Or was it burglars? Or was it . . . ? They crept down the stairs. The kitchen light was on, so it couldn't be the cat. Cautiously, Dad pushed the door wide open and looked in to find . . . not a burglar, but Grisel beside the upended waste bin, picking through a heap of peelings,

13

egg shells, bacon rinds, and tea-bags.

'Darling!' Mum cried. 'Whatever are you doing?'

Grisel looked up, her eyes wide with urgency. And, through the cavernous gap in her upper gums, she whistled: 'I've got to find the toffee wiff my toof before the morning . . . It's worff anoffer *fifty p.*!'

2

Grisel and the School Hat

'Well, nobody told *me* it was Saturday!' Grisel complained, as she climbed into her chair at the breakfast table. The family exchanged glances. It was going to be one of those days! Dad suddenly found himself rather pleased he had to attend a weekend conference; and Hildegard remembered she had promised to go into town with Michelle to help her choose a new dress. And Mum, who wasn't going anywhere, sighed.

Grisel puffed irritably and glared at them in turn. Hildegard – who should have known better – said: 'Well, child, it's quite usual for Saturday to follow Friday.'

'And my teacher says,' Grisel responded, tartly, 'that sarcasm is the lowest form of twit!'

'You mean *wit*,' Hildegard corrected her.

'In her case, I think Grisel got it right the first time,' said Dad. And Hildegard, who was at that difficult age, pushed her plate away and ran from the kitchen, slamming the door behind her.

'Now look what you've done!' said Mum.

'*Me*!' said Dad.

Grisel had this knack of getting everybody at each other's throat. Mum, Dad and Hildegard had been contentedly munching toast, at peace with the world, when Grisel had marched in dressed in blazer, skirt, pudding-bowl hat, and school tie on its elastic outside the collar of her blouse. She wore the uniform of St. Winifred's Primary School under protest; and it had taken some time to master the skills of dressing herself in it. For Grisel was fiercely independent, and only Sister Dorothea, the head-

mistress, could have pointed out that her tie wasn't on properly without there being ructions.

Mum and Dad lapsed into a sulky silence, while Grisel poked her bowl of cereal with her spoon. They were supposed to snap, crackle and pop when you poured milk on them; but, today, the cereal was sulking too.

'Should be back by seven,' Dad mumbled, when he kissed Mum goodbye. He kissed Grisel, too, or at least he tried to, but the hat got in his way. 'You be a good girl for Mummy,' he told her. 'And have a nice day.' This was a saying he had picked up from telephone calls and trips to the United States. But it cut no ice with Grisel. The day had started badly, and she now had a grim interest in seeing just how much worse it could get.

'Are you going to change out of your school clothes?' Mum asked, as tactfully as she knew how.

Grisel gave the question some thought. She disliked the uniform intensely – the elastic in the tie half-strangled her; the elastic holding up the knee-length socks bit into her legs; the elastic in the regulation navy knickers squeezed her tummy; and the elastic of the hat left a mark under her chin.

'Your pink dungarees might be more comfortable,' Mum suggested.

There was, of course, no *might* about it. And, if Grisel escaped from all that elastic into the airy freedom of her dungarees, she would soon feel much better about the world and things in general. But she really quite liked the feeling that everyone and everything deserved a jolly good slapping. And so she continued to spoon cereal into her mouth without answering.

Her breakfast finished, Grisel left the table and stomped up to her room. She would, she had decided, change into her dungarees, *but* she would keep the school hat on. It would be enough to show them she had a mind of her own, and it would remind her that she was in a bad mood; and, at the end of the day, she could make a fuss about the deep elastic mark under her chin. And so Grisel struggled out of the blazer, the shoes, the socks, the tie, the blouse, and the regulation navy knickers. The only thing she kept on was the hat with its stripy band and the badge with the letters 'S' and 'W' twining in and out of each other. Then she stepped into the dungarees, which were soft and roomy. A pair of slip-on sandals completed her weekend costume.

On seeing Grisel and her school hat when she came downstairs, Mum opened her mouth, but shut it again. With Grisel in one of those moods, it was like a storm at sea. All you could do was to batten down the hatches and wait for it to blow over.

For half an hour, Grisel made a nuisance of herself. She stood on a stool and turned the handle of the tin-opener round and round until the screws which fixed it to the wall worked loose and made it wobbly. Then she got the feather-duster and went about the house dusting things so violently that coloured feathers filled the air. Grisel had just begun to pretend that the trolley which held the vegetables was a police car rushing to the scene of a crime, when Mum had a brain-wave.

'Oh!' she said aloud. 'I wonder if it's come.'

Now, if there was one thing Grisel could not abide, that thing was not knowing something. The vegetable trolley skidded to a halt.

'*Wot's* come?' she demanded.

'Lucy's new paddling pool,' said Mum. 'Mrs Turnbull told me it was going to be delivered today.'

There was no need to say more. Grisel abandoned the vegetable trolley and hurried away to push through the gap in the garden hedge to find Lucy-Next-Door. And, in the middle of the lawn, there was a brand new paddling pool. Its bottom was a lovely blue with pictures of fish and shells; and the sides had a pattern of seaweed and sandcastles. Grisel also noted with approval that it was plenty big enough for two. There would be none of that tiresome business of taking turns. Unless, of course, there were three of you. Three was never a good number. Someone always got left out – Grisel saw to that!

But, at that moment, there were not even two of them, for Lucy-Next-Door was nowhere to be seen. Perhaps she was indoors changing. Grisel wished she would hurry up. Waiting was another thing Grisel could not abide. And it would save time, she thought, if the pool was being filled up now. With Grisel to think was to act. She knew where the garden tap was, but she had nothing to carry water in. How very frustrating! And to add to the bothersomeness of things, the elastic of the hat was sawing into her chin. Grisel decided to take the hat off for a minute, while no one was looking.

It was a great relief to be rid of it, and she shook her ginger hair as she dangled the hat by its elastic. And then it struck her. How very like a bucket the felt hat was! And it wasn't as if it could hurt the hat. After all, it was only water. And, as Granny never tired of saying: *Clean water never did anything any harm.* True it would take an awful lot of hatfuls to fill the pool; but at least she could make a start.

Without more ado, Grisel hurried to the tap. As the hat filled, the elastic stretched, and Grisel found she had to put a hand under the hat to support it. Then, when she had a hatful, she carried it to the pool and tipped it in. It did no more than wet a bit of the bottom. She returned to the running tap and filled the hat again. It was on her ninth or tenth trip to the pool that she noticed that water was dripping through the bottom of the hat and that the hat was beginning to lose its hard pudding-bowl shape. And, while she herself was getting very wet, there was less and less water left in the hat to tip into the pool.

On her fifteenth visit to the tap, the hat decided to give up the idea of being a hat altogether; and Grisel found she was left with a soggy piece of felt dangling from a length of stretched elastic, while the stripy ribbon trailed in the muddy lake beneath the tap.

Indeed, although there was very little water in the pool, there was an awful lot of it on the path and beginning to run into Lucy-Next-Door's dad's greenhouse. Grisel thought it might be a good idea to turn the tap off. And it was a very good idea, no doubt about it! So she tried to turn it off with one hand, the other being occupied with carrying the once-upon-a-time school hat. But one hand was not enough. The wretched tap would not budge, and water continued to gush out. Clearly, this would have to be a two-handed job. But what to do with the hat? There wasn't time to find a dry clean place for it; and so Grisel decided she might as well put it on again. It felt quite pleasantly cool; but, instead of sitting stiffly on her head like a helmet, it drooped down over her eyes so that she had to tilt her head back to see what she was doing. Then she grasped the brass handle of the tap with both hands and struggled to turn it. She puffed and strained until her face went purple. And still she could not shift it.

'Oh . . . *bother*!' Grisel exclaimed. '*Bother*!' was a million miles short of expressing how she felt about the tap, but none of Grisel's family used 'lan-

21

guage', and Sister Dorothea certainly did not. Gavin in her class sometimes said *'belly-buttons!'*, but Grisel thought that was simply silly. There must be better words, but, for the time being, she had to make do with *'Bother!'*

And, as she stood there up to the ankles in the torrent which still poured from the tap, she heard voices. Then there was a shriek of horror from Lucy-Next-Door's mum and a squeal of amazed delight from Lucy.

'Grisel! Whatever are you doing?' cried Lucy-Next-Door's mum. And, without waiting for an answer, she hurried to the tap and turned it off. At the same time, Grisel's mum's face appeared

above the hedge, and she, too, shrieked. All this shrieking and squealing left Grisel with nothing else she could do except sit down in the flood and let the world get on with it.

Much later, when Grisel was dried and dressed in clean clothes, Grisel's mum was still trying to get to the bottom of it.

'But I don't understand,' she said for the umpteenth time, 'how your school hat could have got soaked like that.'

Nothing could have been simpler than to explain; but Grisel always felt it showed a lack of imagination to tell the truth.

'It rained,' she said. And then added, 'Hard.'

'Rained!' cried Grisel's mum. 'But nothing else got soaked, except where the tap water flooded.'

'It just rained on my hat.'

'But that's not possible!' Grisel's mum could not hide her exasperation.

'Oh,' said Grisel, without turning a hair, 'I expect it was what Sister Dorothea calls a miracle.'

3

Grisel and the Pantomime

Grisel's class was going to the pantomime, and everyone was thrilled – except Grisel's dad. He complained that the School was always asking him to put his hand into his pocket. If it wasn't for the swimming-pool fund, it was for Sister Agatha's retirement presentation; and, if it wasn't for a minibus, it was for a pottery kiln. 'And now,' he said, 'it's for *pantomimes*!'

'Only for *one*,' said Grisel. She disliked it when people exaggerated to hide their meanness.

'One or twenty-one!' roared Grisel's dad. 'That's not the point! I send my children to school to be educated, not to go to *pantomimes*! I sometimes think that school's nothing but a pantomime!' He would not, of course, have dared to say this to Sister Dorothea's face.

'Well, everybody else is going,' said Grisel. 'Lucy-Next-Door's going. I shall be the only one who's not.' She sighed. 'Still, I expect they'll tell me all about it when they get back.'

She knew perfectly well that, in spite of all the

huffing and puffing, Dad would in the end fork out the necessary cash. But, if he must make a song and dance of it, then she would give him a hard time too.

The pantomime was *Dick Whittington*, and it was being done at the big theatre in town, and there was a special matinée for school parties. Grisel had not been to a proper theatre before and she was looking forward to it tremendously.

The afternoon arrived, and they all lined up in pairs to get into the coach. Grisel's partner was Lucy-Next-Door, and they were going to sit together in the theatre. Their teacher, Sister Agnes, was going with them, and Sister Dorothea herself, and two mums to help out. Grisel saw to it that she and Lucy-Next-Door were at the front of the queue, and they managed to get places just behind the driver. Grisel was to have the window seat going and Lucy-Next-Door was supposed to have it going home.

The journey, though exciting, was uneventful. No one was sick, not even Bernadette Macquire, who was always sick on coaches and who had her very own plastic bucket and sawdust. And, when they arrived, they were all lined up on the pavement again before Sister Dorothea led them up the steps and through the heavy swing doors into the theatre.

The theatre was called The Grand Theatre, and it was very grand indeed. The floor was covered with thick crimson carpet, and the bannisters and chandeliers were all of gleaming brass. The walls were papered in crimson and gold stripes, and there were huge mirrors in elaborate golden frames.

Sister Dorothea said their seats were in the Dress Circle and told them to follow her up the stairs. And such stairs! Grisel felt like a princess going to the ball in Prince Charming's palace. Halfway up, where the staircase turned, stood the statue of a little golden boy who held a lamp, and he had absolutely nothing on. Grisel and Lucy-Next-Door pretended not to notice, but Gavin and Brett got the giggles, and Sister Dorothea had to tell them sharply not to be so silly.

There were rows and rows of seats in the Dress Circle. They were bouncy and upholstered with crimson, velvety material, and hundreds of children all over the theatre were banging their seats up and down and bouncing. Grisel's class was in Row E, and, following Sister Dorothea, they filed along the row until they were told to stop and sit down. Sister Dorothea sat in the end seat next to the aisle. Beside her was Lucy-Next-Door, and beside her was Grisel, and beside Grisel was Brett, and beside Brett was Gavin. This was not a wise pairing of the boys, but on an outing like this even Sister Dorothea wanted all the children to enjoy themselves. And Brett and Gavin intended to do this in their own way, just as much as Grisel intended to do it in hers. For Brett

and Gavin enjoying themselves meant 'mucking about'; for Grisel it meant sweets and drinks. For her, no outing was complete without a good supply of these; and so she had brought to the theatre a bag heavy with toffees, bon-bons and liquorice allsorts, and cartons of juice.

When Grisel had bounced herself breathless on her seat, she decided it was time to make a start on the refreshments. She began with two toffees – two because, if your mouth can cope with two, why not? She began with toffees because they had been strictly forbidden to *drink* anything before the interval. No one was to go to the toilet during the performance, so it was not wise to go swigging Coke or orange juice before. Now, Grisel was very keen on rules for other people, but she did not feel that they applied to her. And so the only problem about drinking now was doing it without being caught. With Sister Dorothea only one seat away, this was out of the question while the lights were on. But, in next to no time, the band began to play, the house-lights went down, and the curtain went up.

Her keen interest in the adventures of Dick Whittington did not make Grisel forget her thirst; and, very quietly, she felt in her bag, poked the straw into a carton of orange, and with a few powerful sucks drained it dry. And Sister Dorothea did not notice. It was a good pantomime, and Grisel shouted and laughed and sang along, enthusiastically. But it was thirsty work, and soon she needed another drink. Within half an hour she had emptied four cartons and was beginning to wonder if, after all, it might have been better if she hadn't. And, as she fidgeted in her seat, she hoped it wasn't long now to the interval.

In the meantime, the pantomime was getting more and more exciting. Dick and his Cat were on a ship sailing away to seek their fortunes when a pirate ship was sighted. The Captain ordered the cannon to be prepared, and then there was a flash and an almighty *bang*! Everyone jumped out of their skin and shouted with surprise and then began to laugh at themselves. Grisel had jumped and shouted with the rest, and she went on giggling with Lucy-Next-Door while Dick Whittington had a sword fight with the pirates. And so it was a little time before Grisel became aware of an uncomfortable damp sensation. She shifted uneasily in her seat, and the dreadful truth came home to her. How wise Sister Dorothea had been! Grisel was paying the price now for those forbidden drinks. And, oh, the shame!

A few minutes later, the curtain fell on Dick Whittington's triumph. The lights went up and the theatre was full of the excited chatter of hordes of children, eager to buy ice-cream, to race about if they were allowed to . . . and to visit the toilets. This was the priority in Lucy-Next-Door's mind, and she was surprised when Grisel said she did not want to go, and hurt and puzzled when Grisel refused to keep her company.

'Why not?' she asked.

'*Because*!' said Grisel; which was what her father always said when he was not prepared to discuss the subject any further. And she sat there, staring in front of her and gripping the arms of her seat. So Lucy-Next-Door left her and followed Sister Dorothea who was shepherding her flock to the theatre loos. Brett and Gavin pushed past Grisel and raced up the aisle, eager to make the most of the confusion and the pandemonium.

And Grisel sat in her seat alone, the only motionless figure in the entire theatre. One of the mums noticed her and came over to ask if she was feeling sick. Grisel shook her head and held the arms of her seat more tightly. She tried to comfort herself with another toffee, but it could not distract her mind from the unpleasantness of wet knickers and the disgrace which must follow on discovery. She hoped that by the end of the performance the lovely, bouncy, crimson, velvety seat would have soaked up most of the moisture.

Lucy-Next-Door came back full of the story that Brett and Gavin had been caught flicking bits of ice-cream with little plastic spoons at one of the ladies who worked in the theatre. Normally, Grisel would have been thrilled. Seeing people she didn't like – and even people she *did* like – getting into big trouble was a treat. But, today, she felt only a flicker of interest at the news. And, when a few minutes later Brett and Gavin were marched back down the aisle by a stony-faced Sister Dorothea, she could not raise a smile. The boys again pushed past her and slumped into their seats. And, then, Grisel heard words which almost made her wet herself a second time.

'Girls,' said Sister Dorothea, 'I must sit next to those two naughty boys, so move this way, please.'

You did not argue with Sister Dorothea. If she said 'Jump', you jumped as high as you could. If she said 'Move this way', you moved that way; and Lucy-Next-Door was in Sister Dorothea's place instantly. But Grisel hesitated. Sister Dorothea, who could make herself heard across a noisy playground without even trying, did not believe that her voice had not carried as far as Grisel, and she was in no mood to be patient.

'*Griselda Sullivan*!' she said.

Keeping her eyes fixed in front of her, Grisel stood and side-stepped into Lucy's place. Then the burly form of Sister Dorothea crab-walked past her and lowered itself into Grisel's vacated seat.

The second half of the pantomime began almost at once, but Grisel's attention was not on the stage. Although she did not dare to look at Sister Dorothea, she was conscious of the headmistress sitting there beside her. And then, after a little while, she heard a creaking as Sister Dorothea began to shift uneasily in her seat. And then she could feel Sister Dorothea's eyes boring into her while she kept her own eyes fixed firmly on Dick Whittington.

At the end of the performance, when it was time to leave, Sister Dorothea did not say anything to Grisel. In fact, she was most unusually silent. But Brett and Gavin spread the story in the coach that Sister Dorothea had wet herself. And they knew that it was true because they'd seen the damp patch on her skirt.

4

Grisel and the Easter Eggs

Grisel was a chocoholic – that is to say, she loved chocolate and could never get enough. And it didn't matter that it made her sick. Throwing-up after she had gobbled a half-pound bar of fruit-and-nut or a whole box of Milk Tray made no difference. It was just *one of those things*. If throwing-up was the consequence of bingeing on chocolate, you had to accept that that was how it was, and make the best of it. But I must not give the impression that Grisel's life was an uninterrupted round of *gorging chocolate – throwing-up – gorging more chocolate – throwing-up again* and so on. Opportunities for hogging chocolate in any quantity were few. The family did not keep her supplied with whole bars and boxes of the stuff, and Grisel rarely had enough cash to buy herself more than a small tube of Smarties.

Now, everyone has a favourite time of year. Christmas comes high in the charts and so do the summer holidays. But, for Grisel, Easter took pride of place, being the one Sunday dedicated to chocolate, the one festival at which the giving and eating

33

of chocolate was something you did whether you liked it or not. Grisel, of course, liked. And, what's more, the chocolate came in egg form; and the chocolate from which Easter eggs are made is the best chocolate of all.

And so, last year, when the snowdrops and aconites began to push their way up through the cold earth, and grown-ups asked each other if they had noticed how the days were lengthening, Grisel looked at the calendar in the kitchen to count the days to Easter. The number was astronomical, and Grisel did not know how she was going to survive chocolate-less for so long. Christmas was the last time she'd thrown-up. Then she had managed to sneak all the chocolate decorations off the tree and eat the lot behind the sofa while the family was watching 'Christmas Night with the Stars'. And she might have got away with it unnoticed; but, when Grisel threw-up, it was always – to use show-biz language – 'a big production'.

As I was saying, the days until Easter seemed endless, and it took all Grisel's common sense to tell herself that each passing was one day nearer Chocolate Egg Day. And so the pages of the calendar filled with the days Grisel had crossed off, until, with less than two weeks to wait, the page with Easter at long last appeared.

At about the same time, the eggs appeared. There were the two Grisel's mum and dad had bought –

one for Grisel and one for Hildegard. Granny's two also came along. And this year Mum's sister, Auntie Vivienne, whom they didn't see very often because she was busy with her career in London, came for a weekend and she, too, brought a couple of eggs with her. So there were no less than six chocolate eggs lined up on the sideboard. They could be admired and desired, *but* they could not be touched before Easter Day.

This put no strain on Hildegard, who was good at waiting. She was also one of those maddening people who could make things last. Not for her a wild orgy on Easter Morning, followed by a sensational throwing-up. Hildegard would be nibbling Easter egg for months! But the sight of those eggs was torment for Grisel. Her longing was so intense she actually dribbled. However, she kept her hands off the eggs, for the threat of their being given away to some poor, deserving children if she tampered with them before Easter Day gave her just enough self-control. So, patiently, she carried on crossing days off the calendar. And all would have been well had it not been for Lucy-Next-Door's Auntie Deborah.

Lucy's Auntie Deborah went to a church with a tin roof, which was very noisy when it rained; but it didn't really matter because the people inside the church were very noisy too. It was just a week before Easter, when Grisel was talking to Lucy, that Lucy said: 'My Auntie Deborah says the world's going to end on Easter Saturday.' Lucy announced this proudly, for not many people have aunties who know things like this. Grisel was rather jealous of Lucy, because Auntie Vivienne could only tell you about marketing computer software. But, instead of getting hot and quarrelling, Grisel went quite cold when she heard what Lucy's Auntie Deborah had said. If the world had been going to end on Easter *Monday* it would have been bad news – but Easter *Saturday*! *Before* she had had a chance to eat her chocolate eggs! This was catastrophic!

Grisel hurried home and stood in front of the sideboard, gazing up at the eggs doomed to perish untasted and uneaten. Her first impulse, of course, was to seize her eggs and devour them on the spot. But she knew her parents would not consider The End of the World a good enough excuse. There would be serious unpleasantness. Grisel looked at the eggs in their shiny foil; and, as she looked, tears filled her eyes. For not only these but thousands of chocolate eggs were going to be wasted, and all because The End of the World could not wait a couple of days. And there was nothing Grisel could do to delay it. There sat the eggs, nestling in the boxes, their plump tummies poking through the cut-out shape which allowed you to see them and, at the same time, held them steady. The eggs were even bigger than they looked because more than half of them was hidden.

Then it was that Grisel had a bright idea. It was not a complete answer to the problem, but it was better than nothing. And she would never have a better opportunity than now to do it, for Dad was out on business; Hildegard was at a friend's, practising flute and violin duets; and Mum had gone upstairs to put in a couple of hours' work on the tapestry she was trying to finish for the Women's Institute Exhibition. So the coast was clear; and, having made up her mind to do something, Grisel did not hang about. It was not her way.

She took down the first of her eggs and very, very carefully undid the box and eased the egg out. She peeled back the foil covering to expose part of the chocolate shell. Then one sharp poke with a stiffened forefinger made a hole so that she was able to break off fragments and pop them into her mouth. So delicious were they that goose pimples ran all the way up the back of her legs. But she did not forget herself. Before the hole she was making became too big, Grisel put the egg back into its box with the damaged portion at the back so that you could not tell that it had been interfered with. She

then repeated the procedure with her second egg, and then her third. The hardest thing each time was to stop breaking bits off.

And then she stood looking at the eggs, pleased that part of them, at least, would not be wasted when the world ended on Saturday. But her lust for chocolate was far from satisfied. And there were Hildegard's eggs. These would be a total write-off. It was so unfair! She longed to do for Hildegard's eggs what she had done for her own; but it was more than her life was worth to meddle with any of Hildegard's things. The fuss there had been over borrowing her frilly ballet skirt when she was playing fairies with Lucy-Next-Door! The tear had been very small and hardly noticed after Mum had mended it. So goodness only knows what Hildegard would do if she found the backs of her Easter eggs had been eaten. And then, of course, it struck Grisel that Hildegard wasn't going to find out. The End of the World wouldn't leave her with any time to bother about Easter eggs.

And so Grisel set to; and, when she had finished, the six eggs again stood ranged along the sideboard. She did feel a touch queasy, but in no real danger of throwing-up, for the bits of chocolate shell she had eaten were very thin, the thick portions, as she knew from experience, being at the top and bottom. But she did go to the bathroom to wash away any tell-tale traces from her mouth and fingers. And no one noticed, guessed or suspected that the eggs were no longer all they seemed to be.

Tuesday, Wednesday and Thursday went by. And then came Friday, the day before the world ended. The family did not seem bothered when Grisel told them that Lucy-Next-Door's Auntie Deborah had said the world was going to end tomorrow. Dad merely grunted: 'I hope it stays nice for her!' But, that night, Grisel made a special point of kissing everyone goodnight – even Hildegard. And she went to sleep hoping The End of the World would be interesting.

The End of the World was very slow in coming. When Grisel woke on Saturday morning, the papers, the post, and the milk had all arrived, but not The End of the World. It hadn't come by lunchtime, and there was still no sign of it when they sat down for tea. Grisel was growing anxious. She had been prepared for anything The End of the World might bring, but not for what would happen if Hildegard found her eggs had been partly eaten. At bedtime, Grisel was quite jittery. Her only hope was that The End of the World could come before the clock struck midnight. So she lay in bed, listening to the clock in the hall. She heard the chimes for nine o'clock before she fell asleep.

Perhaps because she was so worried, she woke early on Sunday morning before anybody else. And everything was as it always was. She looked out of the window, and the world was still there. Lucy-Next-Door's Auntie Deborah had got it wrong! Just wait till she saw Lucy! But what to do *now*? Hildegard was going to find out. It would be ballet skirts with brass knobs on! Now, you will have noticed that Grisel had a logical mind, and even in this crisis she reasoned that if the very worst was to happen because she had eaten *part* of Hildegard's eggs, then nothing worse could happen if she ate *the lot*. Grisel hurried down the stairs.

What the End of the World will sound like when it does come we can only try to imagine; but it is hard to believe that it could sound much worse than the noise which roused Grisel's mum and dad and Hildegard. In their pyjamas, they ran down to the living room where the sight which met their eyes left them lost for words. The floor was strewn with bits of cardboard from boxes which had been ripped open, with cellophane wrapping and with scraps of coloured foil. And, in the middle of it all was Grisel, her face and hands plastered with chocolate, and throwing-up as though she was trying to turn herself inside-out.

'Holy Moses!' gasped Dad, when he had grasped the situation. 'Six whole Easter eggs! The little monster's eaten *six*!'

41

5

Grisel and the Nativity Play

Grisel hated playing second fiddle. If the game was 'Hospitals', *she* had to be the doctor and cut Lucy-Next-Door open; if the game was 'Schools', *she* was the teacher and told everybody off and made them do their work again; and, when the game was 'Fairies and Witches', *she* was the witch, because it is much more fun being really wicked than being ever so good. So, when Sister Dorothea was choosing children for parts in the Nativity Play, Grisel knew the *only* part big enough for her was Mary. Baby Jesus was always played by a doll which spent the rest of the year in a box on top of a cupboard in Sister Dorothea's office. And, in any case, he had nothing to do and nothing to say. Mary was the star part. The year before, Grisel had been cast as one of the angels and all she had had to do was to stand there with all the other angels and not fidget – very boring!

She was, therefore, thoroughly cheesed off when she discovered that this year she was to be only a star – not even *the* star which led the Wise Men to

the stable – just a star. And, when she asked Sister Dorothea what did a star *do* exactly, she was told: 'You twinkle, dear.' Grisel said no more. And Sister Dorothea might have known then from the scowl on Grisel's face that there would be difficulties in coaxing any twinkle from her. Lucy-Next-Door was to be a star as well. But Lucy was perfectly happy to be just one of the crowd, and she would twinkle gladly, if someone would show her how.

The last part to be announced was Mary; and, to Grisel's disgust, Melanie Hubbard got it. Melanie

Hubbard! So she was prettier than Grisel; so she had won a prize for saying poetry; so she did not bite her nails; so she listened carefully to what was said to her; so she was not always getting out of her seat; so she minded her own business – *so what*! The only consolation about not being Mary was that Grisel would not have to put up with that creepy Justin O'Keefe, who was Joseph, putting his arm round her shoulders. But that was a sacrifice she would have made to be centre stage as Our Lady.

Rehearsals began almost at once. Stars had two spots in the show: the first was when the Shepherds are washing their socks by night and the Angel tells them to make a bee-line for Bethlehem; and the second was at the stable where Shepherds and Wise Men and Angels and pretty well everyone are crowding onto the stage to sing 'Away in a Manger'. Grisel felt her part as a star gave her no opportunity to shine. So why, she told herself, should she bust a gut trying to make something of it. She moved where she was told to move, and she stood where she was told to stand. But she did not twinkle. Twinkling, it was explained to them, meant smiling; and Grisel refused to smile. So she looked like the one star in the night sky which had something depressing on its mind.

Stars had no words apart from joining in the carols; but, long before the evening when the nativity play was to be performed for the parents,

Grisel knew every line Mary had to say. Well, she had had to listen to Melanie Hubbard saying them often enough.

'*Oh-Joseph-I-am-going-to-have-a-little-baby-and-his-name-will-be-Jesus.*
Oh-Joseph-I-am-very-tired-where-will-we-sleep-tonight?
Thank-you-Innkeeper-the-stable-will-be-all-right.'

And so on.

Well, Melanie Hubbard might have won a prize for saying poetry, but Grisel did not think much of her performance as Mary. Grisel had seen lots of plays on television where ladies were going to have babies, and they didn't talk like Melanie Hubbard.

And then came the day for trying on the costumes, and everyone was madly excited, because it's always fun dressing up. This was the first year stars had been in the play, and Grisel wondered what they were to wear. She was not best pleased when she found it was a sort of sheet dyed deep blue with a hole in the middle to put her head through. This, she was told, was the night sky. And there was a star shape made out of cardboard covered with silver foil which framed her face. Grisel knew it did not suit her, and far from twinkling her scowl deepened. Even at the final dress rehearsal, when Sister Dorothea called out: 'Now, Stars, *twinkle*, please . . . every one of you!' Grisel's

45

lips were pressed together and the corners of her mouth turned down.

That was in the afternoon. At six o'clock that evening they were back in school to get ready for the real performance. The classrooms where they were dressing and having beards and wings fixed on were full of noisy Shepherds and Angels and Wise Men and Wise Men's Servants, and People-of-Bethlehem, and, of course, Stars, all rushing about getting more and more excited; and there were only about ten minutes before the play was to begin when Sister Dorothea called out: 'Where's Melanie?' And nobody knew. Nobody had seen her. And, just then, Sister Agnes hurried in with the news that Melanie's father had phoned to say that Melanie had been very sick and they thought she was going down with something. They were sorry but Melanie would not be able to go on that night.

'Oh, why,' cried Sister Dorothea, '*why* didn't we get someone else to learn Mary's lines, just in case something like this happened?'

'*I know them.*'

The words were clear, even if a bit whistly, as though the speaker was missing two front teeth. Sister Dorothea looked round to see who had spoken and her eyes came to rest on a lop-sided Star with a freckled face.

'Did you say you know Mary's lines, Grisel?'

'Yes,' said Grisel. ' "*Oh-Joseph-I-am-going-to-*

46

have-a-little-baby-and-his-name-will-be-Jesus. . . Oh-Joseph-I-am-tired-where-will-we-sleep-tonight? . . . Thank-you-Innkeeper . . ." ' And she went on to the end without a mistake.

Sister Dorothea was a headmistress because she could take difficult decisions. She turned to Sister Agnes.

'Tell Sister Cecilia to go on playing carols on her piano-accordion until someone tells her to stop.' Then she spoke to Grisel. 'And we must get you into Mary's costume as quickly as possible. One Star less won't make any difference.' Which was just what Grisel had thought all along!

Grisel was a bigger girl than Melanie, taller and plumper; and so the Mary costume was not a good fit. Sister Dorcas had quickly to unpick a seam at the back of the dress; but the long blue veil Grisel had to wear covered the gap and you couldn't see her winter vest. At last she was ready, and the actors got into their positions on the stage. Sister Cecilia was stopped in the middle of her third performance of 'The Holly and the Ivy'; the curtains jerked open; and the play began.

They often say that good actors are a bundle of nerves. Well, Grisel wasn't. She hadn't a nerve in her body. To be on a stage with hundreds of people looking at her was just great. She adored it. And she was the sort of actor who *lived* her part. Now, this can be a very good thing – up to a point. But

47

plays work because everyone in them knows what is going to happen and what they have to say. That's why you have rehearsals. However, as the nativity play went on, Grisel found it harder and harder to stick to the words she had learnt. She grew impatient with Mary who seemed to let people push her around and that was not Grisel's style at all!

Joseph and Mary had got to Bethlehem and were looking for somewhere to stay. The Innkeeper had just told creepy Justin that they could have his stable for the night, and Mary was supposed to say: *'Thank-you-Innkeeper-the-stable-will-be-all-right.'* But the words stuck in her throat. There was no way Grisel was going to take that sort of treatment lying down.

'*Stable*!' she exploded. 'If you think I'm going to have my baby in a mucky old stable, you can think again!'

The Innkeeper, who had not learnt any other words, stared at her blankly and repeated: *'You-can-have-my-stable-for-the-night.'*

Grisel then rounded on creepy Justin.

'Are you just going to stand there like a pudding? Tell him he's got to find us a nice room with en-suite toilet and bathroom.' And, to add urgency to her demands, she recalled a recent scene from 'Coronation Street'. '*Oooh*!' she cried. 'The baby! . . . It's started!'

At this moment of high drama, Sister Dorothea ordered the curtains to be closed.

Before the final scene – the one where Shepherds and Wise Men and everything came to the stable – Sister Dorothea had words with Grisel. Mary had nothing to say in the scene; she just had to smile. And Sister Dorothea went as far as a holy Sister can to hint that if Grisel uttered so much as *one* word, she (Sister Dorothea) would not be answerable for what she would do to her! Grisel stood through this dressing-down in aloof silence; for Sister Dorothea's displeasure was as nothing compared with the thunderous applause a delighted audience had given her.

6

Grisel and the Orange Drizzle Cake

Grisel's sister, Hildegard, was always winning something or other. The walls and shelves in her room were full of certificates for this and trophies for that. You name it, and Hildegard had probably won it. Grisel had enthusiasm and ambition too, but, so far, the nearest she had got to winning anything was to come third in the Year Three Sack Race. Grisel had had Hildegard's successes up to the eyeballs; and so, when Hildegard got a place in the regional round of the TV competition, 'Junior Master Chef', it was the final straw.

As part of the programme, before the actual cooking began, they spent a few minutes telling you something about each of the competitors; and the television people wanted to show Hildegard at work, cooking for the family. So a day was fixed when a crew would come to do the filming.

Well, the fuss! There wasn't a teaspoon or a meat skewer that had not been polished until it sparkled. New curtains were made for the kitchen, and bunches of fresh herbs and strings of garlic festooned the place. The packets of fish fingers and the bottle of tomato ketchup which were about all that Grisel would ever eat were hidden out of sight. Hildegard would have hidden Grisel too, but the television people had insisted that they wanted to see Hildegard with all her family; and 'a junior female sibling' – which was how they referred to Grisel – would, they said, be good for Hildegard's image as the talented and capable big sister. And that did it! Grisel was blowed if she was going to let herself be used to make Hildegard look like Miss Bloomin' Wonderful! Not even being on television could persuade Grisel to promise to behave as a good little junior female sibling should.

The great day arrived, and the family were up at the crack of dawn to get themselves ready. Breakfast was sandwiches made the previous evening and a thermos of tea, because nobody was allowed into the kitchen which was as spotless as a new operating theatre the Queen was going to open. Grisel – bathed, shampooed, and in her best 'visiting' dress – was forbidden to go into the garden where she was certain to get dirty, or to make a den under her parents' big bed where her dress would get crumpled and dusty, or to play with plasticine which would get under her fingernails.

'So what *can* I do?' she demanded.

'Well,' Mum suggested, 'you could read a nice book, or, perhaps, you could nurse one of

your dollies.'

In her disgust, Grisel did not reply. Never in her life had she nursed a dolly – she had once got into terrible trouble because she had *buried* one. In the end, Grisel didn't really do anything. She just huffed and puffed about the place, getting the ribbon in her hair crooked and getting under everybody's feet; so that, eventually, Hildegard practically screamed: 'What are you doing *there*, child?' To which Grisel responded with dignity: 'Well, I've got to be *somewhere*, haven't I?' But, before Hildegard could go into hysterics, the doorbell rang. *They* had come.

They were the three people in the television unit:

a big, bearded man with a squeaky voice, in charge of lights and the camera; a weedy, little man with a deep husky voice, in charge of sound; and a woman, who seemed to be in charge of the two men and who introduced herself as Melissa.

'Hi!' she drawled. 'Now, *you'll* be Hildegard, the star of the show. And *you'll* be the proud parents. And *this* . . .' She glanced at Grisel and then down at her notes. '. . . yes, *this* will be the little sister. Hi, little sister!'

Melissa made a tour of the house and garden, conferring with Ted and Bob about composition, light and sound balance.

'Right,' she said to the family, 'this is what we'll do. We'll have a shot of Hildegard playing her flute in the lounge – if we move the sideboard and shift the sofa to the other end of the room, it won't look so cluttered. Then Hildegard can sit on the swing in the garden while I chat to her. And, finally, we'll move to the kitchen and get a couple of takes of her preparing . . . what was it? . . . Oh, yes, an Orange Drizzle Cake – *scrummy*!' She turned to Grisel. 'When you're a big girl, you might be able to do clever things like that. Of course, cooking's a gift, like playing the flute. And there's no doubt your sister's very gifted. A difficult act to follow.'

But, first, they'd have an introductory shot, Melissa said, of her arriving at the house with all the family at the door to greet her. After that, it would just be Hildegard on her own. Grisel did not smile in the welcoming shot. Just as well, Melissa thought, as she had caught a glimpse of the horror of Grisel's toothless gums. And after that she did not give her another thought. And she didn't notice that, while Hildegard's parents hung about in the background to watch the filming, the junior female sibling had disappeared from the scene.

Now, the world at large may have thought that Hildegard was the bee's knees, but Grisel thought the world at large did not set high standards. She could see nothing so very wonderful in Hildegard's accomplishments. All right, she had got certificates for playing the flute; but she never played any tunes you'd want to whistle. She did ballet dancing; but anyone could hop about on their toes in a frilly skirt which showed your knickers. And as for being a whizz at sums – well, there were machines which could do that! And it was the same with Hildegard's cooking, really. This Orange Drizzle Cake was a good example. As Grisel saw it, the food-processor did all the work. Hildegard had done so many rehearsals the family was stuffed with Orange Drizzle Cake; and Grisel was convinced that any fool could make one. 'A difficult act to follow . . .' had said Melissa. Her words were a challenge, and, then and there, Grisel decided that she'd show her!

And so, when everyone went into the lounge to film Hildegard tootling one of her Grade Eight pieces, Grisel discreetly slipped into the kitchen and closed the door behind her. On the work surface, everything was laid out in readiness: eggs, orange juice, grated rind, sugar, margarine, flour, cake tin. All you had to do was to tip everything into the mixer – except the cake tin, of course.

The first snag was that the work surface was too high for Grisel, so she dragged a chair to it and stood on that. The second snag was the lid of the food-processor, which she found was very stiff and she couldn't get it off. Her face grew red with the effort, and she called the food-processor a number of unfriendly names before she gave up the struggle. But she was not defeated. The blender stood next to the processor, and its lid popped on and off quite easily. It didn't have all the gadgets the food-processor had, but it mixed things up, which was all that mattered.

The first item in the recipe was three eggs. Grisel took one from the egg rack. She'd watched the way Hildegard broke the shell on the edge of the processor and then emptied the contents into it. Perhaps egg shells are not as tough as they should be; or perhaps Grisel banged her egg down too hard: either way, runny egg white, egg yolk and egg shell spattered the front of Grisel's best 'visiting' dress and puddled the work surface. It was difficult to see how so much egg could have fitted into just one shell. Grisel was annoyed but not discouraged.

56

She selected another egg. Her fingers were still slippery with raw egg, and this second egg shot out of her hand like a bar of wet soap. It rocketed into the air, and then fell back to earth where it exploded on the kitchen floor. Grisel began to form a poor opinion of eggs. Deciding they were unreliable creatures, she took precautions. First, she found a mixing bowl; and then, when she had got another egg, she broke it by banging it in the bottom of the bowl. This time none of the contents was lost; but quite a bit of egg shell got mixed up in it. Grisel repeated the process with a second egg. Since there was already egg in the bowl, it was all much messier this time. And, with the third egg, egg seemed to be taking over. It travelled up Grisel's arms; it made her fringe stand up in spikes where she had run her fingers through it; it smeared her glasses; and more got onto the hem of her dress where she had used it to try to clean her glasses. But, in the end, she had got three eggs, more or less, in the bowl, and she tipped them into the blender.

Grisel was not the sort of cook who clears as she goes, and the dirty bowl and fragments of egg shell and sticky yolk and egg white made the work surface look like the sort of place nice people would avoid. But Grisel pursued her cake-making with enthusiasm. With the eggs attended to, the rest would be easy-peasy. All she had to do was to put the rest of the measured ingredients into the blender. The only snag was that the blender was not as big as the processor and it was harder to tip things in without spilling them.

Grisel started with the easy items. The little bowl of grated orange rind went in without any trouble. So Grisel was not quite as careful as she should have been with the sugar, and some of that sprinkled the sticky egg mess on the surface and some fell on the floor. The margarine would have been all right, except that in the warmth of the kitchen the bits had stuck to each other and to the dish, and Grisel had to use her fingers to get them out, and then margarine seemed to be getting onto everything. But the orange juice was no trouble; and it was only after she had poured it into the blender that Grisel remembered it was supposed to be dribbled over the cake *after* it was baked and to soak into little holes you made with a skewer. Grisel said '*Stocking-tops!*' and then decided it didn't really matter since the juice was going into the cake one way or another. The last item was the flour, and this was a little tricky. It had been standing in a bowl for some time and it had settled; so that, when Grisel began to tip it, the flour did not move. But, when it did, it came out in a rush. A lot went into the blender, but a lot did not, and a cloud of flour dust hung in the air.

Nevertheless, most of the ingredients were in the blender, and all that remained to do was to start it;

and Grisel confidently pressed the switch. At that very moment, Melissa opened the kitchen door and strode in, saying: 'And this is where it all happens.'

How right she was! When you're cooking, it's very easy to forget something. What Grisel had forgotten was to put the lid back on the blender; so that, the instant she switched the blender on, the kitchen was full of egg, sugar, margarine, orange juice and flour. Walls and ceiling dripped Orange Drizzle Cake mixture. And Melissa, who was

dressed fashionably and expensively, gasped as the blender sprayed her soft suede skirt, her pure silk blouse, her West-End hair-do and make-up. When she could see and speak again, what she had to say was not: 'Hi, little sister!' And I have no intention of writing down just what she did say. Enough to tell you that it was much stronger than *Stocking-tops*!

All this was only a matter of seconds; but, by the time Grisel's mum got to the blender and switched it off, the damage was done. Neither kitchen nor Melissa was in any state to continue filming that day. Hildegard burst into uncontrollable sobs; Grisel's father thought bitterly of the time and the expense of redecorating the kitchen. Ted and Bob, who got paid whether or not the job was sabotaged, just shrugged and began to pack up their equipment.

The BBC, it seemed, could not fit another visit into their schedule to film Hildegard in action in the kitchen; and so the world never did see her mixing up a scrummy Orange Drizzle Cake. But it did see Hildegard's family: a proudly smiling father and mother, and a darkly scowling junior female sibling.

7

Grisel and Little Tristram

Before ever she set eyes on little Tristram, Grisel knew in her bones that they would not hit it off.

Little Tristram was the only child of Grisel's mother's old school friend, 'Auntie' Sandra. 'Auntie' Sandra and Grisel's mother had not met for years and years. They had just lost touch, somehow. And then, one day, they had bumped into each other in London; and they'd had *so much* to talk about, *so much* catching up to do! Now they had met again, they said, they really must pick up the threads. And so, a bit later on, Grisel's mother had gone to spend a day at 'Auntie' Sandra's; and, when she got back, she was full of everything, and, especially, was she full of little Tristram.

He was just about Grisel's age. 'Auntie' Sandra had started a family rather late; but, according to Grisel's mother, little Tristram had been well worth waiting for.

'Oh, he's such a *pretty* child!' sighed Grisel's mother. 'Those looks are almost wasted on a boy. He's going to break some hearts when he gets older,

61

you mark my words.'

Grisel, who had already sat through enough of little Tristram to last her for a lifetime, felt more like breaking plates than hearts. But her mother had not yet tired of singing little Tristram's praises.

'And such a *sweet* child!' she exclaimed.

Now, no one had ever, spontaneously, hailed Grisel as 'a sweet child'. Even Auntie Mags, whose religion obliged her to look for the best in everyone, had a real struggle in Grisel's case. But there was no end to little Tristram's virtues. What with little Tristram's manners, little Tristram's thoughtfulness, little Tristram's innocence, and little Tristram's gentleness, Grisel longed to kick little Tristram's shins. And it seemed, if that was what her heart was set on, she would get her chance; for 'Auntie' Sandra was going to return the visit, and she was bringing little Tristram with her.

The day of their visit came and, shortly before lunch, the doorbell rang.

'Oh, that will be them!' cried Grisel's mother, who had spent the whole morning darting about the house, putting finishing touches to things, for 'Auntie' Sandra's house was just about as perfect as little Tristram – who, by the way, never made a scene about putting his toys away when he had finished playing with them. Grisel's scenes when asked to pick up the things she had abandoned in every corner of the house were awesome.

'Now, Grisel, do try to be nice, dear,' her mother said, nervously, as she glanced at herself in a mirror and then hurried to the door, a broad smile of welcome already on her face.

Grisel remained in the kitchen where she was sloshing water over a magic painting book, and her lower lip, which had been jutting out ever since breakfast, was like a doorstep. She heard the squeals of greeting in the hall, the theatrical kisses, and then her mother cooing: 'Hel-lo, Tristram!' and then calling to her as though she didn't know: 'Grisel! . . . Tristram and "Auntie" Sandra are here!'

Grisel stayed where she was long enough for it to be quite plain to the visitors that meeting little Tristram was *not* going to make her day. She had been prepared for the worst, but she was not pre- pared to find that the worst could be quite so bad. What she saw made her think almost affectionately of Brett and Gavin. They were boys and, therefore, they were utterly repulsive. But little Tristram was unnatural. His silky eyelashes alone most girls would have murdered for; and the rest of him was in the same class. He was dressed in designer jeans, designer sweat shirt, designer trainers, and a designer baseball cap. He looked like something out of a fashion catalogue – which, indeed, he was; for he was used regularly as a model. Of course, you can *look* too good to be true and still be quite human in the way that you behave. And, if little Tristram had stuck his tongue out at Grisel or had picked his nose, she might have found it in her heart to tolerate him for an hour or two. But he didn't. Instead, he lisped: 'Hello, Gwithel.' And he gave her the same smile which had sent the sales of Toofy Toothpaste rocketing.

Now, Grisel was not greatly bothered about her own looks. Eyes, she felt, were just for seeing with, mouths for poking food into, and hair to stop you being bald. But, when little Tristram's gleaming smile reminded her of the great gap in her front

teeth, she pressed her lips together in a ferocious scowl.

'She's shy!' Grisel's mother laughed, and blushed because it was such an obvious and whopping fib.

'Ah, the little pet!' said 'Auntie' Sandra, who could afford to feel sorry for all those women who were not the mother of little Tristram.

Grisel continued to glare at little Tristram; but little Tristram only fluttered his eyelashes with his head on one side, the way he had done as Cupid in the TV commercial for *Tell Her With Roses!* It cut no ice with Grisel.

'Lunch!' exclaimed Grisel's mother. 'It's not too early, I think. Just time for a sherry while the spaghetti's on.'

The sherry, of course, was not for Grisel and little Tristram. They had fizzy lemonade with curly, see-through straws so that you could watch the lemonade whizzing round and round on its way out of the glass and into you. Little Tristram took gentle pulls at his as though he were a connoisseur of fizzy lemonade and could probably tell you what year it was and even where the lemons came from. Grisel, on the other hand, drank hers like someone who had been wandering the desert waterless for a week; and, as she drained the last drops, you were reminded of the gurgles when the last of the bathwater goes down the plughole. And you can't drink quantities of fizzy lemonade like that without having a lot of fizz inside you looking for some way to get out again. And so 'Auntie' Sandra had scarcely got over wincing at the gurgles before the room was shaken by a series of volcanic burps.

'Grisel!' her mother remonstrated.

'Can't help it!' said Grisel, and she burped again.

'Well, let's all sit down,' said Grisel's mother, 'and I'll serve up.'

Whatever had possessed her to make spaghetti bolognese? That was the question Grisel's mother asked herself a thousand times after 'Auntie' Sandra had said goodbye and that they simply *must* get together again ... some time. The meal had presented no problems to little Tristram, who knew exactly how to use his spoon and fork to twiddle on just enough spaghetti to put into his mouth. But Grisel's plate and the tablecloth surrounding it resembled a surgical operation performed by a demented butcher. Bolognese sauce spattered the white linen and the front of Grisel's dress. It dribbled down her chin and it drenched her fingers. The spaghetti seemed to have a life of its own; and, at one point, Grisel actually sucked up a long length, which slithered from the heap on her plate like a skinny worm bolting into its hole.

'Why don't you take little Tristram into the garden?' Grisel's mother said to her, when the ordeal of lunch was over.

Well, Grisel *could* have told her! In fact, she

almost said: 'Because little Tristram is less fun than a mouldy prune!' But her mother quickly added: 'There might be some *jelly* for tea.' Next to chocolate, jelly was Grisel's greatest passion. She could bring herself to do almost anything to get it.

'All right,' she said. And to little Tristram she muttered, 'Well, come on then!'

'And play nicely!' Grisel's mother called after her, as Grisel led her visitor from the dining room.

Neither Grisel's mother nor her father was a keen gardener, and they had left the garden pretty much to itself. Shrubs and bushes were overgrown and fruit trees needed pruning. But it was a great garden for playing in, with plenty of places to hide. Little Tristram, however, did not look at the garden with adventurous eyes. He stood, comparing it with the well-groomed garden of his expensive Knightsbridge home.

'Our gardener would have a fit if he saw thith,' he said.

'Why?' said Grisel.

'Well, thith ith just a meth, ithn't it?' said little Tristram.

Only a vision of jelly, gleaming and wobbling on the serving dish held Grisel back from kicking little Tristram there and then. It was a close thing. But she took two deep breaths and then marched to the swing where she often went to let off steam.

This swing was a home-made affair and hung by

whiskery ropes from the branch of a pear tree. Grisel sat herself on it and began to swing and straighten her legs with practised skill, so that quickly she was swinging to and fro and higher and higher, until came the moment when the ropes were almost parallel with the ground, and then, at the end of a forward swing, Grisel sprang into space. For a couple of seconds it was like flying, and then she landed in a squat position. She got back on the swing and repeated the procedure. She was just hitching up her knickers ready for another go, when little Tristram said: 'I want a turn.' Grisel was tempted to tell him he could want; but, again, the bribe of jelly worked its power, and she stood aside for him.

He sat on the swing and waggled his legs, but nothing happened. Little Tristram might be a 'swinger' in the fashion world, but he hadn't a clue about swings.

'Well, push me then!' he demanded. If he had caught the look in Grisel's eye he might have added a 'please'. But Grisel was standing behind him, and he threatened, peevishly: 'If you don't push me, I'll tell Mummy!'

So Grisel gave him a push

'Again!' ordered little Tristram.

Again Grisel pushed him.

'Well, don't stop, thilly!' said little Tristram.

And Grisel didn't. If little Tristram wanted a

swing, he should have one. And the deep satisfaction Grisel found as she pushed little Tristram harder and harder pushed even jelly out of her mind.

'That'th enough now, Gwithel!' little Tristram called; and his hands tightened on the ropes. But Grisel had had quite enough of being told by little Tristram what and what not to do. Each time the swing swung back, Grisel gave it an even harder push and sent little Tristram soaring ever higher. And though he squealed to her to stop and even

added, '*Pleath!*' Grisel was so gripped in a frenzy of *how-high-can-I-push-the-little-toad?* that she was deaf to his appeals.

The first thing little Tristram lost was his designer baseball cap, which was swept from his head as he whooshed through the air. The second thing he lost was his lunch. The good thing about this was that he lost it on a backward swing, so not a lot of half-digested spaghetti bolognese went over his designer sweat shirt and his designer jeans. But little Tristram was in no mood to look for silver linings. His hysterical wails and sobs had a sobering effect on Grisel, who feared, rightly, that all the hullabaloo would bring the grown-ups out to investigate; and she left little Tristram swinging from the pear tree and went into hiding in the bushes, and waited there for the inevitable row. She did not wait long.

Grisel's mother apologised for her at least a hundred times. 'Auntie' Sandra said she was not to worry, but clearly did not mean it. Little Tristram clung to his mother sobbing that that naughty Gwithel had made him get on the swing and then wouldn't stop puthing him. Grisel would not say a word. Little Tristram was cleaned up and had his forehead bathed with eau-de-cologne; and, soon after, 'Auntie' Sandra said that she thought they should be going.

When Grisel's mother had finished waving good-bye and apologising yet again, she turned to Grisel.

'As for you, young lady,' she said, 'there'll be no jelly today. In fact, you'll be lucky if you get any jelly for a month of Sundays!'

And Grisel answered, airily, as though she meant every word: '*I* don't care if I *never* have jelly again in the whole of my life!'

8

Grisel and the Three Wishes

Grisel had always thought that fairy stories were just that – *fairy stories*. Like when she told her mother she hadn't been anywhere near Hildegard's paint box, and had no idea how the yellow ochre had cobalt blue all over it, and how the brushes came to be stiff with dried paint. And her mother had said: 'Don't tell fairy stories!' So, when Grisel found a real fairy at the bottom of her garden, she was surprised and not a little excited.

At the time, she had been playing 'Witches' by herself, and she was poking about in the damp bit by the hedge, looking for toadstools and deadly nightshade so that she could brew a spell to turn Hildegard into a slug. But all she had found had been a toffee paper, an empty snail shell, and a plastic lion which had got lost months ago when she was playing 'Jungles'. None of these was unpleasant enough to turn Hildegard into anything more unpleasant than she already was.

How the fairy let herself be caught is a bit of a mystery, for Grisel was making enough noise to frighten away anything which was capable of moving. Perhaps it was the head cold the fairy was suffering. Perhaps she was so stuffed up and miserable and sneezing and blowing her nose all the time that she just didn't notice Grisel, or anything else for that matter. As it was, when Grisel spotted her, she was sitting hunched up on a small stone. Her wings drooped and her wand was limp. She reminded Grisel of the battered old fairy which was fished out of the decorations box each year and put on top of the Christmas tree. But no sooner had Grisel seen the fairy than she acted. She'd brought an empty yoghurt pot with her to put the spell ingredients in, and this she now whipped down on top of the fairy.

'Gotcha!' she cried.

From under the yoghurt pot came a tiny, stuffy-nose voice.

'Oi! Wod d'you fink you're a-doin' of? ... *Atishoo!*'

'Bless you!' Grisel politely said, but with no intention of letting the fairy go. She had caught grasshoppers and butterflies and small frogs before, but never a fairy. This was something very special and she was going to make the most of it. So she kept her hand firmly on the yoghurt pot while she thought, and while the fairy continued to sneeze and make fluttery noises and, occasionally, yell: ' 'Ere! Stob methin' aboud an' leb me go!'

73

Now, why – you may ask – did not the fairy simply magic herself away or, for that matter, magic Grisel away? I can't answer that. I know very little about fairies. But the fact is that, while Grisel kept her grubby hand on the yoghurt pot, the fairy could not escape. Grisel's problem was that she could not keep her hand on it for ever, and she didn't have a box or anything with a lid she could pop the fairy into. So Grisel went on thinking, and the fairy went on yelling and sneezing until, at last, Grisel said: 'If I let you out, do you promise not to run away . . . or *anything*?' she added, because the fairy might promise not to *run* away and then *fly* away. It is what Grisel would have done in her place. The fluttery noises stopped. Clearly, the fairy was thinking this over.

'Well?' demanded Grisel, who was losing patience. 'If you don't promise, I'll squash you!' This was no idle threat, for – I am sorry to say – Grisel in her time had squashed quite a few small creatures. The fairy must have realised this, for she answered sullenly: 'Oh, all wight, den.'

'Cross your heart and hope to die?' said Grisel.

'Oh! . . Cross my hearb an' hobe to die,' said the fairy. '*Aaaatishoo!*'

Cautiously, Grisel lifted the yoghurt pot, ready to bang it down again if the fairy tried to make a dash for it. But she was still sitting on the stone, resting her chin in her hands, very red in the face, and her

lower lip stuck out just like Grisel's when she was in a mood – not at all like the Good Fairy you see in picture books. She was more of a Cross Fairy.

'Well, leb's ged on wiv it!' the fairy said. 'You've gob three.'

'Three what?' Grisel asked.

The fairy tossed her head and tutted. 'Wod d'you fink?' she snapped. '*Wishes*, moon-face!'

This was rash of the fairy, for Grisel was not the girl to accept insult meekly. But the sudden prospect of three wishes dazzled her.

'An' you've gob to use 'em ub in den minutes,' the fairy said.

Now, this was a new one on Grisel, and she thought the fairy might be bluffing. She said so. 'You're bluffing,' she said.

'Amb I?' said the fairy. 'Try me! Id's no skin ob my dose!'

Three wishes are three wishes, and Grisel did not want to risk losing them just to prove a point, so she thought quickly.

'Right,' she said. 'Turn my sister, Hildegard, into a slug.'

'You mus' be jokin'!' the fairy protested. 'In *my* condition!' She sneezed again and swabbed her nose with a hanky which was already like a wet dishcloth. 'You neeb to be on peak form for a job like that. Fink again, sweethearb! . . . *Durn my sisber indo a slug!*' she muttered contemptuously. 'Some beoble 'aben't gob the brains wod they wos born wiv!'

'Well, what *can* you do to my sister?' Grisel asked.

'I can gib 'er a cold in the 'ead.'

This was a bit of a comedown, but better than nothing, Grisel decided.

'All right, then,' she said. 'Give my sister a cold in the head.'

'Okay,' the fairy snuffled. 'Well . . . ? Leb's be 'abin' number two. You ain't god all day. In fac', you'b only god sebben minutes.'

76

Grisel thought desperately. There were hundreds of wonderful things she would like to ask for; but, if the worst the fairy could do to Hildegard was to give her a cold, it seemed unlikely that she could transform St. Winifred's School into Disney World or make Grisel fly. It was hard to think of things for magic wishes as small as colds in the head. It then occurred to Grisel that on Monday Sister Agnes was going to give the class a multiplication-tables test. Grisel wasn't any good at tables. They bored her, and Grisel refused to waste brainpower on things which bored her. But neither did she like not doing well in tests, especially when Lucy-Next-Door was sure to get full marks. Grisel almost wished to know the tables but, just in time, she thought of a better solution to the problem.

'My wish Number Two,' she announced, 'is to miss school on Monday . . . You can do that, can't you?'

'Standin' on by 'ead,' said the fairy, although she stayed sitting on her stone.

Only one wish left and the minutes racing by. Really, thought Grisel, she hadn't got much for her first two magic wishes. Of all the fairies in the world she was dead unlucky to catch this one. And all that sniffing and sneezing was getting on her nerves. It stopped her thinking.

'Oh, I wish you'd stop all that sniffing and sneezing!' she snapped.

Too late, she clapped a hand over her mouth. Too late! She'd done the same stupid thing people were always doing in fairy stories.

'I didn't mean . . .' she began to say. But the fairy only grinned and stuck out her tongue at Grisel.

'Sucker!' she jeered, without a trace of cold. And vanished.

Grisel searched about a bit in the bushes, but without much hope of finding the fairy. And the more she thought about what had happened, the more cross she became. All she'd got were two measly little wishes out of three. Just her luck!

She did perk up a little at tea time when Hildegard started to sneeze and her nose began to drip. Mum took her temperature and packed her off to bed. This was nowhere as satisfying as seeing Hildegard turned into a slug; but it was something to know that her first wish had been granted. It gave her great hopes of Number Two. And, sure enough, Grisel did miss school on Monday. She was in bed with the cold she had caught from Hildegard. Her head ached; her throat was sore; and she could not stop sneezing.

After school that evening, Lucy-Next-Door was allowed to visit her for just a few minutes if she didn't get too close. Lucy-Next-Door was very sympathetic.

'And you missed the play,' she said.

'Wod play?' sniffed Grisel.

'Students from the College came and did this play about a magician and monsters and things. It was ever so good. You'd have loved it, I know.'

The fact that she would have loved it did not make Grisel feel any better about having missed it. But she forced herself to look on the bright side.

'Ad leas' I missed the dables dest,' she snuffled.

'Oh, no!' Lucy-Next-Door exclaimed. 'There were so many people away with colds, Sister Agnes said she'd wait until you all got back again.'

It was then that Grisel vowed that, if she ever caught another fairy, she'd squash it on the spot.